Woodland Magic

DEER IN DANGER

D1457047

THE WOODLAND MAGIC SERIES

Fox Club Rescue
Deer in Danger
The Stranded Otter

Look out for more adventures to come!

Woodland Magic

DEER IN DANGER

JULIE SYKES
illustrated by KATY RIDDELL

Piccadilly
PRESS

First published in Great Britain in 2022 by
PICCADILLY PRESS
4th Floor, Victoria House, Bloomsbury Square, London WC1B 4DA
Owned by Bonnier Books
Sveavägen 56, Stockholm, Sweden
www.piccadillypress.co.uk

Text copyright © Julie Sykes, 2022
Illustrations copyright © Katy Riddell, 2022

A CIP catalogue record for this book is available from the British Library.

ISBN: 978-1-80078-143-6
Also available as an ebook and in audio

1

Typeset by Envy Design Ltd
Printed and bound in Great Britain by Clays Ltd, Elcograf S.p.A.

Piccadilly Press is an imprint of Bonnier Books UK
www.bonnierbooks.co.uk

For Antoni, Will and Tim with love
and a sprinkle of beach magic!
J.S.

To Harry.
K.R.

Chapter One

'There's nowhere to sit. Let's try upstairs.'

Cora looked around the Crow's Nest, a two-storey treehouse cafe perched at the top of the tallest oak in the Whispering Woods. It was full of chattering Keepers, hungry after working in the Big Outside.

Cora and Jax climbed the twisty wooden staircase wrapped around the oak tree's sturdy trunk. Stepping out onto the top floor, Cora stood for a moment, enjoying the gentle rocking sensation as the tree's branches swayed in the breeze. The cafe was

less crowded up here. Spotting an empty table next to the viewing platform, Cora rushed over. She wriggled out of the straps of her woodland bag. The bag was empty now, except for Cora's tools, and she dumped it on the floor. Jax shed his bag and slid onto the bench opposite her. His eyes shone.

'Work was fun. I love rewilding in the Big Outside. It's much more exciting than school.'

'Much!' said Cora. 'The Big Outside is enormous, and I love the wild animals, like those badger cubs we saw today.'

Cora and Jax had been sent to work on a stretch of wasteland behind a Ruffin factory. The ground was hard and bare and nothing grew there. But on the way they'd crossed an allotment and seen badger cubs playing in the orchard.

'Imagine living back in ancient times, when badgers and other wild animals freely roamed the countryside and dug it up,' said Cora. 'The earth would have been soft enough for wildflowers and grasses to grow without our help.'

Jax sighed. 'And there'd have been more time for collecting the things we need.'

'Like the magpie feathers.' Cora had been thrilled when she'd found them. They were black and white with a shimmery line of blue.

Scarlet was delighted too. She said she'd use the feathers to make a fan to help keep the school cool in the summer.

'We're still on trial though,' Cora added. She had hoped that the feathers and the work they'd done in the Big Outside today would have been enough for Scarlet to make them fully trained Keepers. But it hadn't.

'Scarlet still doesn't trust us!' said Jax.

Cora nodded. It was true. At first, she'd thought that it wasn't her fault – trouble followed them around. But it didn't. Trouble happened when she and Jax got distracted by other things.

'We've got to work even harder and never mess up again or Scarlet will definitely send us back to school.' Anxiously she asked, 'You want to pass your trial, don't you?'

'Of course! I love the Big Outside. I want to look after it and help nature to recover

from the Ruffins. And I'd like to teach
the Ruffins how to be more careful with it,'
Jax added.

'Jax!' Cora gasped.

The Ruffins were huge, giants really.
They could flatten a Keeper with one stamp
of their pongy feet. Keepers mostly avoided
them by only working in the Big Outside
before sunrise or after sunset. As well as caring
for the countryside, the Keepers lived off it
too, collecting things to wear, use and eat.
'*From nature's floor to our door,*' as Scarlet was
fond of reminding everyone. Scarlet was in
charge of the Keepers. She set them tasks to
complete in the Big Outside and gave them
Wants, a list of the things that were needed.
Scarlet was also responsible for the stores,
where everything they collected was kept.

Jax grinned. 'Think about it. Easier for
us if we don't have to keep fixing things

for the Ruffins. If we helped them to look after their home, then maybe they'd help us back.'

'How? By not eating us?' said Cora darkly.

'That too!' Jax pulled a stone dice from his pocket. He rolled it across the table. 'Want to play six high?'

'Sure!' Cora snatched up the dice, but before she could roll it, Nis and Trix arrived with trays of woven grass loaded up with plates and cups.

'Buttercup doughnuts with nettle cream, and daisy smoothies all round,' said Nis.

'Fresh today – that's why it took so long. Everyone wanted them and there was a huge queue,' said Trix.

Nis pulled a face. His dad was the cook. 'Dad wouldn't let us queue-jump, even though the nettle cream is made with the plants we collected yesterday.'

At the sight of the delicious snacks, Cora forgot about the game and threw the dice back to Jax. He caught it and shoved it in his pocket.

'Yum, my favourite. Thanks, Nis.' Cora took a doughnut and bit into it. Nettle cream oozed over her long fingers.

'Eew! Look at Cora, all covered in cream just like a little baby.' A superior

voice floated across from another table.
'No wonder she's still only a *trainee*.'

Cora's cheeks burned as she turned to
see Penelope Lightpaw, or Perfect Penelope,
as Cora secretly called her, and her best
friend Winnie watching her. The two
friends dissolved into giggles.

'Not fair,' she muttered, pretending to
ignore them as she licked the cream away.
'Penelope only passed her training because
Winnie helped her. She's very lazy – she bosses
Winnie around and lets her do all the work.'

'It won't be long before you pass the
training,' Trix soothed.

Cora shot Trix a grateful look. It was all
she'd ever wanted, to become a fully trained
Keeper and to work in the Big Outside,
caring for the countryside, making sure
that every animal had somewhere safe to
live. Cora loved wild animals more than

anything – except for her mum and her best friends, of course.

'Are you hungry?' Cora asked Trix as she demolished her doughnut in three bites.

Trix grinned. 'Scarlet's invited me to the workshop later to help her with the new car, but first I have to help Signor Dragonfly perform a school experiment.' Clever Trix, who wore her purple hair in a bun skewered with a tiny screwdriver, loved science and engineering.

Grandmother Sky, the ancient Queen of the Hidden Middle, had been finding it hard to move around recently. Building her an environmentally friendly car had been Scarlet's idea. It was the first car the Whispering Woods Keepers had ever had. The car's maiden trip would be to transport Grandmother Sky to the river for her birthday regatta in the autumn.

Trix drained her smoothie. 'Scarlet's worried that the car won't be ready in time.' Trix was at her happiest tinkering around in Scarlet's workshop, often with smears of acorn oil over her hands and face.

'You'd better hurry,' said Cora.

'Hurrying!' Trix drained her daisy smoothie and stood up. 'Catch you later.'

'I'm going to paddle in the brook. Anyone else?' asked Jax, as they waved goodbye to Trix.

'Me!' shouted Cora and Nis.

'Race you there!' Jax jumped up and, grabbing his woodland bag, ran to the twisty chute, the fast and fun way down from the top of the oak tree to the ground.

Cora hesitated. Jax was full of fun ideas that sometimes got them into trouble. But right now there was nowhere else she needed to be. She leapt up and chased after him and Nis.

Then someone said crossly, 'Cora Swallowtail, stop right there!'

Chapter Two

Cora pulled up immediately as Scarlet's voice cut across the cafe.

'Cattywumps!' she whispered. What had she done wrong now?

'Aren't you forgetting something?' Scarlet had arrived for a break, just as Cora and her friends were leaving. She balanced her tray, laden with food, on the table where Cora had been sitting and plucked something from the ground. It was Cora's woodland bag.

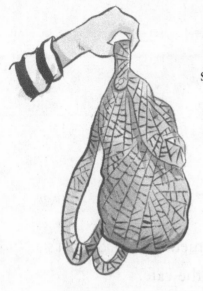

Cora's face flamed redder than a poppy as she slunk back to fetch her bag. Everyone was watching and she felt their disapproval. Penelope could barely contain her laughter. A woodland bag was the most important part of a Keeper's kit. It was made from spiders' thread and infused with magic so that it could carry anything without breaking it, no matter how big or heavy the thing. It could even hold a Ruffin, if you were brave enough to catch one. How could she have forgotten it?

Scarlet's eyes held Cora's as she handed the bag over. 'You must pay more attention, Cora. Do not forget this again.'

'I won't,' Cora promised, annoyed with herself – she was supposed to be proving to Scarlet that she was responsible enough to be a fully trained Keeper.

Jax and Nis were waiting for her at the top of the chute.

'Bad luck. Trust Scarlet to catch you,' said Jax.

Cora shrugged. She knew luck wasn't the problem. She only had herself to blame for leaving her woodland bag behind. She climbed onto the chute and sat for a second, looking out over the leafy green canopy of the Whispering Woods. The Hidden Middle, where the Keepers lived, was surrounded by a thick bramble hedge. Cora loved gazing at the fantastic houses hidden behind it. Keepers were very creative, and their houses had turrets, towers, tall chimneys

Woodland Magic

and twisty steps that blended in with their
surroundings.

Grandmother Sky's enormous palace
was Cora's favourite. It was set amongst the
spreading branches of an ancient beech,
in a clearing in the centre of the Hidden
Middle. Pretty flower-petal flags flew from
the palace's many turrets, and its wooden
staircase, that spiralled around the outside of
the tree's trunk, was decorated with garlands
of ivy. The Crow's Nest, at the top of the
tallest oak tree, was opposite the palace
beech. A brook ran through the clearing,
passing the Big Barn, where the Keepers
gathered for celebrations and special events.
A wooden bridge spanned the brook, and
amongst the branches of a sycamore tree
was Cora's old school.

'Snoring boring!' Cora muttered
quietly. She couldn't get sent back there!

She wanted to be having adventures in the Big Outside.

'I'll pass my training and become the best Keeper ever,' she vowed. Cora wrapped her arms around her woodland bag and, clutching it tightly to her tummy, pushed herself off. Her green hair streamed behind her and everything whirled as she followed Nis and Jax, round and down the twisty chute.

The next day, Cora woke extra early before dawn. After sharing her breakfast of bark-bread toast with Nutmeg, her tame mouse, she hurried down the staircase that twisted around the trunk of her treehouse. At the bottom, she waited for Jax, hopping on and off the bottom step when he didn't arrive on time. A while later, Mum squeezed past her. She didn't go rewilding much these days as she worked at the Crow's Nest. Cora

didn't understand it. She loved her home
in the Hidden Middle of the Whispering
Woods, but how could her mum not want
the thrill of being in the Big Outside?

'Stay safe, keep out of sight and don't get
caught by the Ruffins,' Mum said, waving as
she hurried to the cafe.

Impatiently, Cora
waited for Jax. At
last he appeared
at a run, his long
blue hair whirling
around him, wilder
than a tornado.

'I overslept!'
he panted.

Cora tried not to be cross. 'Jax, you
acorn! We're supposed to be making a good
impression and getting to the Bramble
Door early.'

Cora's woodland bag bounced against her back as they raced for the door in the thick bramble hedge surrounding their village.

To Cora's annoyance, they arrived just behind Penelope and Winnie. Penelope was half asleep and didn't look pleased to be going to work, but she brightened at the sight of Cora and Jax.

'Hello, *trainees*,' she said loudly. Looking pointedly at Cora's messy green hair, she ran a hand through her own neat pink locks. 'Do you think you can manage on your own in the Big Outside, or do you need a fully trained Keeper like me to help you?'

Cora breathed deeply.

'Ignore her,' Jax whispered. 'She's only trying to wind you up.'

'She is!' It wasn't fair. Without Winnie's help, Penelope would still be a trainee.

Penelope sniggered, but she wasn't smiling when Scarlet gave her and Winnie a long list of rewilding jobs.

'Since you're fully trained Keepers,' Scarlet said sweetly, her lips twitching as she fought back a smile.

Then it was Cora and Jax's turn.

Scarlet consulted her list. 'A new housing estate is being built on the edges of Sunny Meadow and Downy Woods. The houses are stopping the hedgehogs who live there from roaming as far as they need to find food, to nest and have babies. Your task is to create a hedgehog highway by making holes in the garden fences that are blocking the hedgehogs' way.' Scarlet tapped her pencil on her list. 'This is a big and important job. It will be very hard work and you will need to focus. Do you think you can manage, or should I give it to someone else?'

'We'll do it,' said Cora immediately.
She loved hedgehogs, with their whiskery
faces and bright eyes. Why couldn't the
Ruffins share the Big Outside with the
wildlife instead of building huge fences
that kept everything out! Perhaps Jax was
right and the Ruffins did need the Keepers
to show them how to look after the
countryside!

'We will,' Jax agreed.

'Hmmm.' Scarlet frowned. Cora smiled
hopefully until Scarlet's face softened. 'Good.
I'm trusting you not to let me down. My

Wants today are: fallen petals, to make
garlands for Grandmother Sky's birthday
regatta, and Signor Firefly needs dandelion
seeds, for the nursery school.'

'Petals and dandelion seeds,' said Cora,
stepping closer to the door.

Scarlet raised a hand to stop her. 'Wait
for the Warning: *Stay out of sight and don't get
caught by the Ruffins.*'

'We will – I mean, we won't,' said
Cora hastily.

Scarlet nodded, and with the Want and
the Warning delivered, she let them pass.

Cora felt a fluttering of excitement as
she hopped through the Bramble Door. It
was always the same, no matter how many
times she ventured out into the Big Outside.
It was an adventure waiting to happen.

'Come on!' she told Jax. 'We'd better
get going. There's a lot to do.'

They set off, running through the woods, leaping over gnarled and tangled tree roots. In the spooky pre-dawn light, the trees reminded Cora of ghosts. She almost screamed when Jax stopped suddenly at a prickly bush beside a creepy-looking tree.

'Fur,' he said. He teased a ball of red-brown fluff from the thorny bush.

'Deer!' said Cora admiringly, as Jax shrugged off his woodland bag and carefully stowed the fur inside. 'Good find.'

They went on, reaching the edge of the Whispering Woods in record time and crossing over the river by the arched footbridge. They passed the boatyard and its cafe, then hurried over the football field to the play park. Here, only last week, they'd completed their first task, to sow wildflower seeds on the ground around it. Cora and Jax stopped to admire their work.

'Look how much the flowers have grown. They're taller than us now!' Cora exclaimed.

Helped along by a sprinkling of woodland magic, the once barren ground beside the play park was now a riot of colour, with bright yellow buttercups, purple-pink comfrey, frilly knapweed, bluebells and fluffy white dandelions all jostling for space.

'Dandelion seeds,' said Cora. She stood on tiptoes to blow on the dandelion clocks.

Jax blew with her, until finally the ripe seeds detached from the plant heads and drifted around them like furry snowflakes.

Cora and Jax chased the seeds, catching them in their cupped hands and stowing them in their woodland bags.

'No fallen petals yet,' said Jax, searching the ground.

'If we can find some petals, that would be two things on Scarlet's Want List. We might even pass our training today. Imagine that!' said Cora, determined to keep a lookout for petals.

They continued on, passing the primary school and skirting around the village, where they entered Sunny Meadows. The long grass towered above their heads. It was heavy with dew and speckled with wildflowers. Cora and Jax had to push their way through a jungle of stems. Soon, Cora's clothes were soaked through. She didn't mind. Running was hot work and a dew-drop shower was very refreshing. Cora kept a keen eye on the

ground, hoping to find petals. Surely there
would be some when the grass was bursting
with so many wildflowers. Then the forest of
stems suddenly ended. Cora drew up sharply
with a gasp.

Chapter Three

'Nooo!' she wailed. She stared at the dusty, bare ground in dismay.

Once, the flower meadows had continued right up to Downy Woods. Now a large area of flowers and grass had been cleared to make way for new houses and roads. Some of the homes were finished, others were still being built. Trenches, marked with rope and pegs, showed where more houses would go.

'What have the Ruffins done?'

'They have to live somewhere,' said Jax reasonably.

'Why are their houses so huge?'

'Ruffins are huge. Look at their enormous machines. You could knock a whole forest down with any one of those.' Jax pointed to a collection of diggers, dumper trucks and cement mixers parked together by the unfinished houses.

'Looks like they already did.' Cora pointed to a pile of tree trunks, stacked in a pyramid-shaped pile.

Nearby, the roped-off trenches were surrounded by a flimsy metal fence secured by concrete blocks. Cora thought it looked ugly.

'Why do the Ruffins make so much horrible stuff?'

'Maybe they like it,' said Jax.

At the furthest end of the meadows, a row of finished houses stretched all the way to the edge of Downy Woods. Once the woods had been open to the meadow, but now a tall wooden fence separated it from the homes.

'Ruffins love their fences,' said Cora.

The individual gardens were also separated by tall wooden fences that went right down to the ground. Some of them had gates, but there were no gaps for a hedgehog to wriggle under. The house fronts were even less wildlife-friendly, with tarmac-covered drives. Every house had at least one car parked outside it.

'Ruffins love their cars,' said Jax.

Cora felt a sudden pip of worry. 'Cattywumps! I didn't realise it would be this bad! What were the Ruffins thinking? Don't they ever wonder what will happen to the wildlife? Making a hedgehog highway through that lot will take us for ever!'

Jax pointed at the row of huge metal machines. 'Not with those. If the Ruffins stopped to think about the wildlife's needs, they could build a highway in a mouse blink.'

Cora shook her head. 'Their machines are too big to make hedgehog holes.'

Jax stared longingly at a squat dumper with a huge scoop at the front. 'Imagine riding one. I bet they go really fast.'

'Jax, no!' Cora stood in front of Jax as he took a step closer. 'Fluff head!'

Jax blinked, then smiled at Cora innocently. 'Acorn brain! You didn't think I would, did you?'

Cora grinned back. They both knew that Jax was a daredevil. She wouldn't have put it past him to climb up onto a Ruffin machine for fun.

'Let's get started on the highway.'

They walked along a new road to the first house in the row, side-on to the woods . Cora hated the feel of the tarmac under her feet.

'Poor hedgehogs. There's no way through at all. Let's build the highway right at the end of the gardens where the Ruffins are less likely to notice it.'

'Or us while we're working,' said Jax cheerfully.

Cora glanced up nervously at the back of the houses. She could only see the upper parts, but they were all in total darkness. Hopefully that meant that the Ruffins were asleep. She shed her woodland bag and emptied out her tools, eager to finish the job quickly, before the Ruffins woke. Cora selected a hand drill, a small saw and her favourite green pencil, made from a stick infused with mint.

'Stand there!' she told Jax.

Obediently, he stood against the forest fence while Cora drew a green arch around him.

'My turn.' Jax stepped back and, taking his hand drill, made a hole at the bottom of the arch, big enough to get a saw through.

Together, Cora and Jax slowly cut around the arch shape. Sawdust rained over them, turning their grass shirts white and making Cora sneeze. At last, it was done.

'Now for the fun bit,' said Jax.

Standing side by side, they pushed on the arch shape, almost falling through the hole when the wood popped out.

Cora brushed more sawdust from her shirt. She collected up her tools and popped the wooden arch into her woodland bag. Keepers never left a mess and Scarlet would find something clever to do with the arch-shaped pieces.

'One hole!' said Cora, trying not to think about how many more they had left to cut.

'We should try it out.' Jax ducked through the hole into the woods and back again.

'Perfect!' said Cora. She glanced at the upper windows again. They were still in blackness. There was no putting it off. It was time to make a start on the Ruffins' gardens.

Chapter Four

Cora stood against the next fence while Jax drew an arch around her.

'My favourite part!' he said, picking up the drill.

They were faster cutting the second hole. Jax darted through it. Cora followed, her eyes widening at what she saw. The garden was bare, there were no bushes, no plants, just a strip of grass that wasn't even real. The fake grass ended in a paved area at the back of the house. The blackened windows seemed to Cora like giant watching eyes.

'Let's be quick,' she said, but as she reached down to pick up the cut-out wood, a light snapped on, filling the garden with a white beam.

Cora's heart leapt like a grasshopper. She jumped back, flattening herself against the fence.

'Freeze!' she hissed.

'Frozen!' said Jax.

Cora stood in the shadows, her back pressed to the fence panel, hoping that she was too tiny to be noticed.

'Can you see a Ruffin?' mouthed Jax.

Cora couldn't, unless one was hiding, biding their time, ready to pounce when Cora and Jax moved.

She cupped a hand to her pointy ear, grateful that her hearing was much sharper than the Ruffins', with their funny rounded ears. Immediately, Cora heard the near-silent pad of paws crossing the lawn. Relief flooded her.

'It's a cat! It must have triggered the light.'

A large ginger and white tabby sauntered along the garden.

'Shhh,' breathed Jax as the cat came closer.

Cora remained stiller than pondweed trapped in ice. They weren't out of danger yet. Cats weren't as bouncy and scary as dogs, but it was better not to attract their attention. They loved to chase, and if they caught you, they always wanted to play. Playing with a cat was like wrestling with a hedgehog. Cora's mum knew – she'd been scratched by one once. The cat came closer. Cora held her breath. Had the creature seen them?

Suddenly it sprang. Cora's heart thundered against her chest. A tail sailed over her like a furry banner. Paws scrabbled as the cat landed

on top of the fence and balanced there. A second later it was gone, disappearing into the next garden as it jumped down. Cora's breath rushed out noisily.

'Close!' said Jax, looking pale.

'I hope it doesn't come back.' Cora hadn't reckoned on interruptions. The hedgehog highway would take even longer to build at this rate, and they had to collect

some more stuff for the stores. A ball of fur
and some dandelion seeds, even though they
were on the Want List, wouldn't be enough
for them to pass their trial. Cora had hoped
to search for fallen petals in Sunny Meadow
on the way home. The light switched off,
plunging the garden back into darkness.
Cora gathered her things up to cross over to
the opposite fence, but Jax stopped her.

'We're not done here yet.'

'Aren't we?' Cora looked round in
surprise,

Jax frowned. 'It needs something else.
This garden is so bare. Fake grass, no plants
or bushes. What's to stop the Ruffins
from seeing a new hole in their fence and
blocking it up again? They won't know
it's a hedgehog highway. What if they fix
the hole and then come looking for the
thing that made it? Us!'

It was a startling thought.

Cora stared at Jax. 'What are we going to do?'

Jax fell silent. Finally he said, 'We could make a flap to cover the hole, like the ones the Ruffins have in doors for their cats.'

'Flaps need hinges. It'll take us ages if we have to make them,' said Cora. 'How about we disguise the holes instead? We could grow some real grass. We can get seeds from the woods. Think how good it'll be for the insects too. We can use woodland magic to make it grow faster.'

Woodland magic was a gentle magic, not strong enough to zap a Ruffin and turn him into a squidgy cowpat, but it was still very useful.

Jax's eyes shone. 'We could plant the dandelion seeds we collected too. Dandelions make great cover.'

Cora's stomach squirmed like a compost heap full of earthworms. It was a great idea, if only dandelion seeds weren't on Scarlet's Want List!

Jax guessed her thinking. '*From nature's floor to our door. Caring for the countryside and taking only what we need*,' he reminded her.

Jax was right. Caring for the countryside came first, always. Only then could they take what they needed from it.

'Dandelions seeds it is,' she agreed.

They nipped through the hole to the woods and collected grass seeds. Back in the garden, Cora and Jax dug up the earth around the fence, rubbing it into the freshly cut wood to help disguise it. They planted the grass and dandelion seeds on either side of the hole. Then it was time for some woodland magic, Cora's favourite part.

Standing together, she and Jax pointed their long fingers at the ground and zapped it with a magical mist.

The mist sparkled, fizzed and popped. Cora shut her eyes and pictured the grass and dandelion seeds growing tall and strong.

A high-pitched squeak startled her eyes open. She jumped back as tiny green blades of grass and dandelion shoots broke through the ground and shot up around her. Dandelion leaves began to unfurl, knocking Jax over. He landed on his hands and knees, bottom in the air. Cora doubled up laughing, then suddenly she was flying through the air, batted over by another uncurling leaf. She heard Jax giggling. It was infectious. Cora laughed till her stomach hurt. Jax came over and gave her a hand to get up. Together they admired their handiwork.

'Perfect!' said Jax.

It was, but it was also a long slow task.

Cora glanced at the sky. Her face creased with worry. 'What if we don't get it finished in time?'

'We will!' said Jax.

They ran across the garden to the next fence. They didn't chatter like they usually did, but worked silently to get the job done. A few fences later, Cora's arms ached from all the sawing. She was also keeping an anxious eye on the grass and dandelion seeds.

'What if we don't have enough?' she asked.

'We'll go to the woods and get some more,' said Jax.

Still Cora worried. They needed things to take back to the stores. Scarlet wouldn't be happy if they came home with empty woodland bags.

'We're nearly done now,' said Jax at last. 'Three more fences, and there'll still be time to forage for stuff on the way home.'

Cora felt like dancing when they reached the last fence. The task was nearly complete. She and Jax cut the final hole and planted the last of the grass and dandelion seeds around it.

'We should test the highway before we leave,' said Jax. He packed his tools away and hitched his woodland bag onto his back.

Cora agreed. 'We'll use it to cross the gardens.'

'Race you. Hi, lo, go!' Jax sprinted away,

leaving Cora still wiggling into the straps
of her woodland bag as she went after him.
Jax burst from the last hole a pip in front
of Cora.

'I won!'

'You had a head start,' said Cora. Her eyes
shone. 'That was great fun. The hedgehogs
should be very happy with their new
highway. Now they can roam freely between
the woods and the meadow.'

'It was brilliant,' said Jax. 'Want to do
it again?'

Cora hesitated – she did. She'd loved
racing Jax and she wanted a chance to
beat him, but there was something else that
she wanted more desperately. For Scarlet
to make her a fully trained Keeper. 'Another
time. We should collect some stuff for
the stores.'

'OK!' said Jax.

They started across the housing estate, going back over the tarmac road to the Ruffins' machines. Dust motes whirled in the air as something rushed their way. The shape moved silently. Cora and Jax drew back, hiding in the shadow of a dumper truck.

'Deer!' said Cora admiringly, as the shape solidified into a young male deer with tiny three-pronged antlers. 'Something's spooked him.'

As the deer raced by, Jax gasped. 'He hasn't seen the fence!'

'Stop!' shouted Cora. Waving her arms, she jumped out of her hiding place to try to warn him.

It was useless, she was much too small. The deer didn't see her and rushed on!

Chapter Five

Cora covered her face with her hands,
watching between her fingers. At the
very last moment, the deer saw the fence
and jumped. Cora glimpsed hooves and rust-
brown fur. A few seconds later, she heard the
clatter of Ruffin metal and a loud crash. A
panicked screech pierced her ears and then
it went silent.

Cora and Jax ran over. The flimsy metal
fence, held up with the concrete blocks, had
broken. A large section lay on the ground.

The fence was made up of small metal rectangles. Carefully, they jumped across it.

'Where did the deer go?' asked Jax.

'Over here.' Cora reached a piece of pegged string and ducked under it. Weirdly, she was now on the same level as the deer's head. She looked again. The rest of the deer was trapped in a deep trench. The deer's nostrils flared. He trotted forward until he reached the end. There was no way out.

The trench's sides were too steep to climb and there wasn't room to jump.

'Stay still!' Cora couldn't bear to see the deer's distress as he scrabbled to be free.

Jax came up beside her. 'Is he hurt?'

Cora shook her head. 'I don't think so, but he's terrified. I'm going to help him. Hold onto me.' Cora waited for Jax to put his arms around her waist, then leaned into the trench. She stroked the deer's reddish brown shoulder. 'Hello, you,' she said softly.

The deer stared up at Cora with huge, frightened eyes. He arched his back and kicked out, trying to break free.

'Stay still. You're going to hurt yourself.' Cora stretched out her fingers and sprinkled the deer with woodland magic. It crackled from her fingers and fell in sparkles on the deer's back. Cora imagined him floating out of the trench.

The deer snorted in surprise as he began to rise up from the ground. Cora held her breath – was her woodland magic strong enough? It wasn't. An eye blink later, the deer's hooves hit the ground with a soft thud. Cora frowned, dragging her hands through her hair as she tried to recall some of the more useful things she'd learned at school.

'Remember that lesson with Signor Dragonfly when we made that pulley and a sling to lift each other over the brook?'

Jax chuckled. 'We were racing with Trix and Nis, only we crashed into Perfect Penelope. Everyone fell in the water and Penelope got tangled in starwort.'

'Not that bit,' said Cora, grinning at the memory of Penelope with mud dripping down her face, her perfect pink hair turned green with the starwort. 'The bit when we made the pulley. What did we use?'

Jax scratched his head. 'A grass blanket, sticks, woven vines and a small wheel, I think.'

'Could we make something similar to winch the deer out?'

'It might work,' said Jax. 'But what would we use?'

Cora and Jax searched the immediate area, looking for things both natural and

Ruffin-made. Cora found a thick plastic bag caught beneath the wheel of a cement mixer. The bag was empty except for a few particles of sand stuck to the inside. Nervously, she approached the machine, not trusting it to stay still, even though Signor Dragonfly had told them that Ruffin machines needed a special key to make them work.

The bag felt nasty. Cora gritted her teeth as she pulled on it. At first it didn't budge, but at last she felt the plastic give. Jax came over to help her. With the extra pair of hands, the top of the bag thinned and stretched, leaving the remainder firmly trapped beneath the giant wheel.

'Stuck fast.' Jax panted. 'We'll have to find something else.' He stood back with his hands on his hips and stared up at the machine. 'If only we had a Ruffin key.

We could use the dumper truck to lift the deer out with the scoop.'

'Too dangerous!' said Cora firmly. She was suddenly anxious that he might climb up the machine and find its key. 'The machine's so big. We could hurt the deer if we got it wrong.'

Cora had a plan. She glanced around. The sky was grey and silent. She couldn't hear any birds bringing in the dawn with their noisy chorus. If she was quick, there was enough time to put it into action.

'I'm going home,' she announced. 'I'll ask Scarlet to lend me something from the stores to make a pulley and sling so we can lift the deer up out of the trench.'

'Want me to wait with the deer or come with you?' Jax asked.

'Come with me.' Cora smiled at him gratefully.

Jax was a brilliant friend. They both knew
it was far too dangerous for him to wait on
the Ruffin building site alone.

Before starting back, Cora and Jax
checked on the deer. He was rocking back
and forth, trying to get up the momentum
to leap out of the ditch.

Cora sprinkled him with more woodland
magic. It spluttered from her fingers and
she flexed them in dismay. Woodland magic
wasn't that strong, and she'd used lots of

hers already. She probably needed a rest.
Luckily, the extra magic was enough to
calm the deer again. Cora felt happier about
leaving him.

'We're coming back,' she promised.

The deer's ears twitched and swivelled her
way. Cora leaned into the ditch and stroked
his head. Then she and Jax took off, running
across the building site until they were back
in Sunny Meadows. Petals and seeds rained
on Cora's head as she pelted through the tall
grass and flowers, but she couldn't stop to
collect them! Cora and Jax ran on until they
arrived back at the Bramble Door, hot and
out of breath. There, they startled the elderly
Keeper guarding it while everyone was
working in the Big Outside.

'Cattywumps!' he exclaimed, almost
falling off the log he was sitting on. 'Why are
you back so early?'

'We're not exactly back!'

There was no time to explain, not if they wanted to rescue the deer and forage for useful stuff. Cora and Jax rushed on, stopping only when they reached the stores.

They stood outside for a pip, clutching each other for support as they caught their breath. When they stepped inside, the stores were empty. Neither Scarlet nor her assistant, Haru, were working behind the long wooden counter.

Cora stared round the empty chamber in disbelief.

'Helloooo,' she called. 'Where is everyone?'

Jax slipped behind the counter. 'Not here!' he said, boldly continuing towards the passage at the back. 'We'll have to help ourselves.'

'Jax . . .' Cora started.

No one was allowed in the stores without
Scarlet's permission. Scarlet could send
them back to school for breaking that rule.
Then again, if they wasted time searching
for her, they might not make it back to the
deer, help him out of the trench and get
home before sunrise, when the Bramble
Door would be locked. Anyone not back
by then was stuck in the Big Outside. The
locked-door rule was never broken, to keep
everyone safe from the Ruffins.

Cora went behind the counter and
followed Jax into the main tunnel. The stores
were simple in design. A winding tunnel
ran down the centre, with smaller tunnels
branching off that led to various chambers.
Here, in the chambers, Scarlet and Haru put
everything that the Keepers collected when
they were out rewilding in the Big Outside.
Some of the things in the stores had been

there for ever and used many times, like the ancient aurochs horns, the flints and the mammoth tusks.

Cora loved visiting the stores, she'd been several times when at school, but being there without permission made her insides wriggle like a maggoty apple. Ignoring her worries, Cora followed Jax as he darted in and out of chambers, searching every single shelf. It was dusty work, sifting through feathers, fur, flowers, twigs, fungi, leaves, animal bones and teeth.

'There has to be something here we can use,' said Cora in despair.

Jax darted into yet another chamber, this one much larger than the rest. Cora followed him and gasped in surprise. They were in Scarlet's workshop. In the middle stood Grandmother Sky's shiny new car.

'It's beautiful!'

Cora hadn't expected the car to be so
grand. Its wooden bonnet was polished
like a mirror. Its roof, made from bright
green leaves, was folded back, but it could
be pulled over in cold weather. The car had
long running boards, huge wooden wheels
and moss green seats. Proudly, Cora took in
the eggshells used to make the headlights,
eggshells that she and Jax had collected.

'I wonder how fast it goes.' Jax stepped closer.

'Jax, don't touch!' Cora was suddenly scared that if they so much as breathed on the car, they would be in huge trouble. Scarlet had a way of knowing things. 'Anyway, what about the deer?'

Reluctantly, Jax came away. At one end of the workshop was a stone table with chairs, carved from tree trunks, set around it. A collection of tools was laid out on the table, along with scraps of fur and plants. One of the chairs was pushed back as if someone had left the table in a hurry.

'So, we're in Scarlet's workshop,' said Jax. He pounced, scattering tools as he snatched up a green bundle. 'This is perfect!' He held out a rope ladder made from the brown tops of bulrushes and bound together with vines.

'Hopping hares!' said Cora. Their luck was in. She imagined herself climbing down the ladder to wrap a sling around the deer. 'We could use this too.' She scooped up a patchwork blanket made from scraps of fur. Cora recognised fox, squirrel and stoat. The fur scraps had been dyed with juices from berries. Cora loved the colourful mix of red, yellow, green and blue.

Jax nodded his approval. He sorted through the tools and picked up a round wooden bobbin with a thread of spun fur attached. 'We'll take this as well, and some of the leftover bulrushes and vines. They might come in useful.'

They stowed the things in Cora's woodland bag. Heading out of the stores, Cora half expected to see Haru or Scarlet back at the counter. It was spookily quiet though – even as they hurried to the

Bramble Door, they didn't see anyone.
Most of the Keepers were still at work in
the Big Outside. Cora was encouraged.
It meant that there was still time to help
the deer.

Chapter Six

On the way back, Cora worried that her woodland magic might have worn off. She couldn't bear it if the deer had injured himself trying to escape. The thought spurred her on and she ran extra fast, Jax hurtling along with her. They arrived at the new housing estate out of breath. Cora had a stitch.

'Jumping jackdaws, you were fast!' said Jax admiringly.

Cora didn't have enough puff to answer. She stood panting and clutching her

stomach until her breathing slowed. Then
she checked on the deer. He was beginning
to grow restless. Hurriedly Cora shrugged
off her bag and took out the ladder, blanket,
bobbin, vines and bulrushes.

'Now what?' Jax asked.

Cora thought back to the pulley and
sling they'd made in school to cross the
brook. 'We need to attach some vines to
the blanket.'

'Easy squeezy!' said Jax.

Only it wasn't. Neither Cora nor Jax
had scissors so they had to make holes in
the blanket with their drills before they
could attach the vines. Cora's first hole
was too near the edge of the blanket and
when she threaded the vine through the
hole, it broke. Jax made two more holes,
both too big, and they broke too. By the
time they'd worked out how far away

from the edge to make the holes, the blanket looked like it had been eaten by hungry moths.

What would Scarlet say about that? Cora wondered as she and Jax tied the vines to it.

The next problem was making a pulley.

'We can use the bulrushes and the bobbin,' said Jax, propping three long bulrush stems together to make a triangular frame, which he secured by tying them with a vine. But each time he tried to fix the bobbin to the frame, the tripod collapsed.

Cora glanced up. Had she heard a tweet? Surely the birds weren't awake already! She listened anxiously, aware that the sky was much lighter now. But no, she'd been mistaken. She turned back to the tripod problem. How would Trix solve it?

'What if we put stones around the base?' she suggested.

There were plenty of stones around of all different sizes. Jax found half a brick and together they carried it over. Cora gave the wooden frame a hard shove. To her relief, it didn't budge.

'That should do it. Next we have to get the sling around the deer.'

The deer was young, but so much bigger than them. Putting a sling around him would be dangerous. He could easily crush a Keeper if he moved at the wrong time.

'I'll do it,' said Jax bravely.

'No, me!' said Cora. 'Pleeeasy squeezy!'

Jax gave in. 'We need to secure the rope ladder first.' He went over to the pyramid-shaped wood pile and returned with two sturdy sticks. Pulling a hammer from his woodland bag, he hammered the sticks a few times until they stood up in the ground at the top of the ditch. The deer flinched.

'It's OK,' Cora soothed him.

When Jax was done, he hung the ladder from the sticks and lowered it into the trench. Cora stood at the top, looking down. Her stomach was at it again, hopping around like frogs.

'Hand me the blanket when I say,' she said bravely.

She turned round and grabbed the top of the ladder, her foot feeling for the first bulrush tread. She was about to put her full weight on it, when a shout made her hesitate.

'Stop!'

Trix and Nis pelted across the building site, their woodland bags bouncing on their backs. 'Do not use that ladder!'

Trix got there first. 'It's not secure.' She picked up Jax's hammer and bashed each twig, forcing them further into the ground. 'That's better. They would have come out when you put your weight on the ladder.'

Cora and Jax exchanged a look.

'Close one!' mouthed Jax.

Cora nodded. Thinking about what might have happened made her shiver. 'Is the rest of it OK?'

'Good to go,' Trix agreed.

A thought occurred to Cora. 'Were you on your way home?'

'Yes,' Trix said. 'We've finished our task.'

'Ages ago,' added Nis. 'We were planting grasses on the other side of Downy Woods, to provide the owls with somewhere to hunt for food. We saw an owl too – it swooped over us just as we were leaving. Then we went into the woods and gathered mushrooms and wild garlic. Dad said if we found both, he'd make pizza for the cafe.'

'Yum!' Cora was momentarily distracted.

'Mushroom and wild-garlic pizza!' Jax rubbed his tummy.

Trix walked around the pulley system attached to the wooden tripod, her eyes narrowed. She examined the blanket and tugged at the vines attached to it. Trix patted her bun, looking for her screwdriver. She pulled it out and a few strands of purple hair fell around her shoulders.

'Screws,' she muttered, delving into a pocket and bringing out a handful of wooden ones. 'Just a few tweaks,' she explained vaguely as she set to work on the tripod. 'You've done a good job, but this will make the pulley run more smoothly.'

Cora waited nervously, her eyes flicking between the deer and the sky – it was

growing lighter by the minute. What was
Trix doing?

'There. All done!' Trix stepped back at last
and admired her handiwork. 'It pivots now,
and that will allow us to move the deer away
from the trench before we lower him to the
ground. It's lucky we arrived when we did,'
she added. 'A deer weighs millions of pips.
You're going to need our help to lift him.'

Cora set off down the ladder, her
confidence growing with every step as it
held firm. She could hear Jax, Trix and Nis
talking in soothing voices to keep the deer
calm. There wasn't much room in the trench.
Carefully, Cora squeezed past the deer and
put the blanket around him, using a small
sprinkling of woodland magic to help her
get it under his belly and up the other side.
Her magic was much stronger after a rest.
Nis ran around the trench to catch the edge

of the blanket as Cora fed
it through.

Job done, Cora
climbed back up the
ladder while Nis
attached the ends of
the vines to the pulley,
giving them a tug to
make sure they were properly
attached. Cora, Jax, Trix and Nis
crowded around the pulley and
each took a strand of the vine.

'Ready? Heave ho, GO!' Cora shouted.

Everyone pulled together. The vines
creaked as they tightened, taking the
weight of the deer and raising him up. The
deer gave a surprised snort as his hooves
left the ground. For a moment everyone
stopped, holding the deer aloft as they
caught their breath.

'Again!' Cora said.

They heaved again. The deer was much heavier than Cora had imagined. Grinding her teeth together, she hung on to the vine and ignored the burning sensation in her arms. The vines were moving. The deer rose slowly up from the ditch, his long legs dangling.

'We've got this!' Jax shouted encouragingly.

Cora pulled harder, her eyes crossing.

'We're almost there,' Trix called out. 'Careful now, while we swing him round.'

Cora and her friends took tiny steps, moving with the deer as he swayed overhead. Wrapped in the blanket, suspended from vines, he looked like a monstrous beast cocooned in a spider's web.

'Down,' said Trix.

Slowly they lowered the deer to the

ground. Cora and Jax ran forward, hacking at the vines with their saws. The moment the deer was free from the sling, they ran like hares back to Trix and Nis, watching from a safe distance.

For the briefest of seconds, the deer locked eyes with Cora. *Thank you*, he seemed to be saying. Then, with a snort, he sprang away, galloping to the woods where he melted into the trees.

'Yay!' cheered Cora, crossing her hands and holding them out for a celebratory spin.

Jax, Trix and Nis came forward, crossing their arms, joining up in a circle and holding hands. With joyful whoops they spun around until suddenly the roar of a car engine made them break apart. Car wheels crunched on loose stones and a blinding light fell on Cora, fixing her to the spot.

Chapter Seven

'Ruffins!' shrieked Trix. 'Hide!'
Everyone scattered as they searched
for the nearest hiding place. Temporarily
blinded by the light, Cora didn't move.

'Cora, run!' Jax, Trix and Nis shouted
at her.

She snapped out of her trance. Arms
pumping, she fled. Her friends reached the
dumper truck and disappeared under its
scoop. The car lights bore down on Cora.
She changed direction, knowing that if she
followed the others now, she'd give away

their hiding space. An abandoned bucket
lay on its side. Cora headed towards it.
Jumping over the handle she dived inside
and immediately tripped up. She shrank
back and looked to see what she'd stumbled
over. *A nose!*

The nose twitched, sneezed and
withdrew. A dark shape moved, rolled up
and turned into a gorse bush. Cora rubbed
her arm where it had caught her. She
observed the prickly ball from a distance.
It was a hedgehog!

The roar of the car's engine stopped.
A door creaked open.
Hiding in the
bucket with the
hedgehog, Cora
heard two
Ruffins
talking,

a man and a woman. Their voices were
almost as loud as their stonking great feet.

Cora wriggled deeper inside the bucket,
crouching behind the spiky hedgehog ball
as the footsteps came closer. Two pairs of
booted Ruffin feet appeared at the bucket's
edge. A torch light shone inside. Cora
remained frozen, hoping that her pounding
heart wouldn't give her away.

'I saw them, plain as the nose on my face.
They ran in front of the car,' a gruff voice
said. 'One definitely went this way.'

'Fairies!' scoffed a higher voice. 'How old
are you?'

'They were small enough to be fairies,'
the gruff one insisted.

Fairies! Cora was outraged. She only just
stopped herself from shouting back at the
Ruffins, *We're Keepers, not fairies!*

The Ruffin's knees cracked as he squatted

down. Cora covered her ears. Ruffins were
too loud, even the little ones. This one
was very scary. He was by far the biggest
Ruffin Cora had ever seen. Not that she'd
seen many. Most Ruffins were tucked up
tight in their houses when she visited the
Big Outside. This Ruffin had a beard and
he wore a yellow vest that glowed in the
torch light.

Cora, half blinded by the light and the
vest, shut her eyes and held her breath, just
in case his rounded ears worked better than
most Ruffins'.

'Well I never! I did see something.' The
Ruffin's voice boomed around the bucket.

Cora nearly fainted with fright. Had he
seen her? She was also worried about the
hedgehog. They didn't like loud sounds
and Ruffin voices could make them
anxious. A long time ago, Ruffins used to

bake hedgehogs in the oven and eat them.
Cora didn't think they ate them nowadays,
they ate Keepers instead, but perhaps the
hedgehog didn't know that? There was a
rhyme about it. The words ran through
Cora's head.

> *'Fee fi fo fum, I smell the blood of Jack*
> *Keeper. YUM!*
> *Be he alive or be he dead, I'll grind his*
> *bones to make my bread.'*

The rhyme came from an ancient book
called *Nursery Rhymes*, found by one of
the Keeper's ancestors. Most of the book
was too damaged to read, but all Ruffins
knew that *Nursery Rhymes* was a copy of the
Ruffins' rules written in verse for children.

Cora clamped her teeth together to stop
them from chattering in terror. Who would

be there for Mum and Nutmeg if the Ruffin caught her?

'Aww!' The other Ruffin had a long dark plait that fell over her shoulder. 'I haven't seen a hedgehog in years. Should we move it somewhere safer?'

'Not likely! Hedgehogs are full of fleas! Anyway, we've got to start work. Come on.'

The torch beam swung away and the Ruffin with it. The other Ruffin took one last look in the bucket then, with a sigh, followed.

'Acorn head!' Cora exclaimed.

Hedgehogs' fleas only lived on hedgehogs and never on stinky Ruffins or their bouncy, pouncy cats and dogs. Every Keeper knew that, even the babies in Signor Dragonfly's nursery class. Cora waited in the bucket until she heard car doors slam and the roar of an engine. She slipped round the rolled-up hedgehog and peered out of the bucket in time to see the Ruffins slowly drive to a fenced area on the other side of the building site. Now they'd tidied their car away, they would probably come over on foot for their machines.

The bucket rocked. Cora spun round to see the hedgehog uncurling. As it stretched out, its long spines shot at her like spears. Cora leapt out of the bucket before she was skewered. The hedgehog ambled after her. It sampled the air with its black button nose before moving away, walking briskly in the direction of the woods. Cora watched, fascinated. Would the hedgehog find the hedgehog highway, or would it need a sprinkling of her woodland magic to give it a helping paw? And what about Jax, Trix and Nis? If the Ruffins were heading for their machines, then she needed to warn them.

The hedgehog was moving further away. Cora scanned the area while listening with her sharp ears. She couldn't hear Ruffin footsteps yet. If she was quick, there was time to follow the hedgehog and then warn her friends. She ran after the hedgehog, catching it up as it approached the first fence. Cora hung back, nervously bouncing on her toes. The hedgehog missed the hole and stopped halfway along the fence. Inquisitively, it sniffed it. Cora held her breath and hoped that it would realise there was a route through.

'Cora! *Thank the forest!*'

Jax, Nis and Trix arrived next to Cora. The hedgehog froze, ready to curl up in a protective ball. Cora, finger to her lips, nodded at it. Silently, everyone crowded closer to watch. The hedgehog grew more confident. It took a hesitant step forward, then another. Growing bolder, it shuffled along the garden, following the fence. Cora held her breath, willing it to keep going.

'Come on, hedgie, just a few more steps,' she whispered.

And then the hedgehog was there. With a happy grunt, it stuck its nose through the hole. Its body followed. There was just enough room. As its spiky bottom disappeared, Cora beamed at Jax. Tapping her thumbs together she said, 'Well done, us!'

'Yay! Well done,' Jax whooped, tapping his thumbs back at her.

Trix fell on Cora and hugged her. 'Don't ever scare us like that again!' she scolded. 'When the Ruffins shone their torch in the bucket, we thought you were bark-bread toast!'

Jax nodded vigorously. 'Toast!' he agreed.

'They were the scariest Ruffins I've ever seen!' Nis added. 'Those horrible glowing vests.'

'The hedgehog saved me,' said Cora. 'I hid behind it and the Ruffins didn't see me.'

'That's because they never look at anything properly!' said Trix scornfully.

'It's time to go home,' said Nis. 'It's almost sunrise.'

'What about the blanket and ladder?' asked Cora, determined not to forget anything after almost losing her woodland bag in the cafe.

Jax banged his palm to his forehead. 'Cattywumps! That's the Ruffins' fault. We didn't have time to pick them up.'

They returned for their equipment. Cora tidied it into her woodland bag while Jax, Nis and Trix checked around to make sure they hadn't left anything else behind. From the woods, a bird called out. After a pip, a second answered. It wouldn't be long before more joined in, welcoming the dawn with a noisy chorus of song. Cora sighed. The shift had gone too quickly. They'd finished their task, but with the dandelion seeds used up, they only had the clump of deer fur for the stores.

Jax guessed what she was thinking. 'We'll keep a lookout for something on the way back. There might be some fallen petals.'

Cora hoped so. They started jogging for

home, but as they approached the Ruffin machines, one of them roared into life.

Cora shrieked, her cries drowned out by the throb of the machine and the rattle of the digging tool attached to the front. The digger lurched closer. She changed direction, running away from the machine's huge wheels, swerving again when it followed her. Had the Ruffin driving it seen her? Cora couldn't be sure, but it wasn't stopping so maybe he was deliberately trying to flatten her.

'Nearly there,' Cora shouted to her friends. She could see the long grass of Sunny Meadows just ahead. The machine was so close its deafening roar was making Cora's ears ring. Would she reach the meadow, or would she be flattened like a berry in a smoothie? Cora leapt the last few steps, her lungs burning, and landed in a clump of wildflowers. She pressed herself into their tall green stems and was joined by Jax, Trix and Nis.

'Too much running!' Cora panted.

'Way too much,' said Jax.

They peeped between the flower stalks, watching as the machine rumbled along, suddenly changing direction again as it headed for the parcels of land marked out with string and freshly dug trenches. Cora took a deep breath, trying to replace the stinky machine smell with the sweet scent of meadow flowers. Her heartbeat slowed. Calmer now, she looked about her for fallen petals. A long way off, a horn sounded.

Cora's eyes met Jax's. 'Tyr!' she said.

Chapter Eight

The Horn of Tyr, an ancient Viking horn, was used to call the Keepers home. There was nothing for it – they had to get back before the Bramble Door shut. Hurrying through the meadow alongside her friends, Cora mentally ran through the contents of their woodland bags.

Jax had the clump of deer fur. She had nothing except for the borrowed blanket, *now in tatters*, the ladder, *dirty*, the remains of the vines and bulrushes and the wooden arches. Every last dandelion and grass seed they'd collected had been used up to hide the hedgehog highway. She hadn't found any spare petals. There was nothing special like woodland garlic or tasty mushrooms to show Scarlet.

Would the work that they had put into building the hedgehog highway be enough to keep her happy? It might, thought Cora optimistically, but only if Scarlet was in a *very* good mood.

As Cora, Jax, Nis and Trix entered the Whispering Woods, they joined a procession of Keepers, all with bulging woodland bags on their backs. They walked quickly, overtaking the slower ones, including Penelope and Winnie. Meanly, Cora couldn't help wondering if Penelope had actually done any work, or whether she'd left it all to Winnie, as usual. Scarlet was at the Bramble Door, counting the Keepers in as

they returned from
the morning shift.
She nodded at Cora
and Jax, eying them
thoughtfully as they
stepped through
the doorway and
into the Hidden
Middle.

Cora's chest
tightened and her
heart flapped like a
bird caught in a net.
It felt like Scarlet
knew that she hadn't collected anything
for the stores. Cora thought about asking if
she could go out again later with the night
team, who worked from dusk to moonlight,
but Scarlet was busy counting more Keepers
in and the moment had passed.

'That's all of you!' Scarlet waved the last few stragglers home, slamming the Bramble Door behind them.

The lock creaked and, looking back, Cora saw Scarlet pop a wooden feather-shaped key into the front pocket of her dungarees. She strode towards the stores, overtaking Cora, Jax, Nis and Trix with her long easy stride.

Cora and her friends had to join a trailing line of Keepers outside the stores. Nervously she waited as the line shuffled forward. In a peck it would be her turn to have her woodland bag emptied. The line seemed longer and slower than usual, and when Cora finally made it inside the stores, she saw why. Haru was alone at the counter. From the chambers at the back, she could hear someone muttering and banging around. It sounded like Scarlet. What was she doing?

At last, Trix and Nis reached the counter and Nis emptied his woodland bag before Haru. Snatching up the wild garlic, his wrinkled face brightened with a smile.

'Mmmm! It smells delicious. And mushrooms, lovely, Nis. I shall look forward to eating them in one of your dad's wonderful creations. Poppy petals too. Scarlet will be pleased.' He broke off, wincing as an extra loud crash came from the stores.

'Is everything all right?' Trix asked Haru as she emptied her woodland bag out.

Haru glanced over his shoulder into the tunnel that led to the stores, then, turning back, he said gravely, 'Scarlet was working on a couple of things when Signor Dragonfly asked her to assist him in a science lesson. When she returned, the things had mysteriously disappeared.'

Cora listened, her stomach tightening like bindweed.

Haru continued. 'The bulrush and vine ladder was almost ready to be installed in a new playhouse for the nursery children. The blanket was to keep Grandmother Sky warm when she drives her car to her birthday regatta.'

'Cattywumps!' Cora mouthed to Jax. She'd never have taken the blanket if she'd known it was for Grandmother Sky.

With legs wobbling like frogspawn, Cora stepped forward and turned her bag upside down on the counter.

Haru stood very still. 'Ah!' he said eventually.

'I didn't mean to damage them. There was a deer. It was stuck in a Ruffin's hole.'

'Foundations,' said Trix. 'The deer fell into a trench that the Ruffins had dug for

their new houses. We used the blanket and
the rope ladder to lift him out.'

Scarlet chose that moment to return.
Spying the tatty blanket and the ruined
rope ladder, she let out a gasp. 'What is the
meaning of this?'

Cora explained again, in a tiny voice,
what had happened.

Scarlet's eyes narrowed. 'You took these items from the stores without asking my permission. You damaged them almost beyond repair. And what about the Wants? Have you brought anything back for the stores?'

'Deer fur,' said Jax, reaching into his bag and pulling out the small clump.

'A tiny ball of fur.' Scarlet exhaled slowly, her nostrils flaring. 'One reason,' she said in a low voice. 'Give me one good reason why I shouldn't send you both back to school?'

Cora's legs trembled. She'd never seen Scarlet so angry. Would she have helped the deer if she'd known how much trouble she'd be in now? Then she remembered how terrified he was and his grateful look when they'd freed him. *Yes!*

'The hedgehog highway,' Trix piped up. 'Cora and Jax completed the whole thing. We even saw a hedgehog. The poor creature was wandering around the new housing estate until he found the highway. We watched him use it to get to the woods.'

Scarlet was taken aback. She looked from Cora to Jax. 'You rescued a deer *and* you finished the hedgehog highway? All in one shift?'

Cora and Jax nodded.

'And we found the fur,' Jax added.

'Poppy petals!' said Nis suddenly. Reaching forward, he pulled two bright red petals from Cora's hair.

Cora was amazed. Petals were on Scarlet's Want List. Had they got caught in her hair when they'd run through the flowery

meadow? Or had Nis just put them there?
Nis smiled innocently. Cora smiled back,
suddenly feeling more hopeful.

'We'll fix the ladder and blanket, Jax and
I. Please don't send us back to school,' she
blurted out.

'Hmmm,' said Scarlet. A long silence
passed. Then, 'Go!' she said at last. She
flapped her hands at Cora and Jax, shooing
them away. 'Come back when everything is
mended. Be quick.'

'Going!' said Cora, almost forgetting to
pick up her woodland bag as she gathered
up the blanket and ladder and hurried
outside with Jax.

Cora hadn't got far when she heard
someone calling her name. It was Trix
and Nis.

'We'll help you,' said Trix, running to

catch up. 'You and Jax start on the blanket.
It needs a wash in the brook before you
mend the holes. Nis and I will repair the
bulrush ladder.'

'Really?' For a peck, Cora was tempted
by Trix's offer. Fixing the ladder would be
tricksy. Cora's brain ached just thinking
about it. Whereas mending the blanket
would be fun, especially splashing around in
the brook with Jax while they cleaned it.

Trix held out her hand for the ladder.
Cora hesitated. She would never match
Trix's brilliance or passion for making and
repairing things, but she'd never learn to do
anything for herself if she always let Trix do
it for her.

Bravely, Cora shook her head. 'Thanks,
but we can manage. Meet you at the Crow's
Nest later. Save us some seats.'

Trix looked like she was about to argue. Then she grinned. 'Don't be long. Come and find me if you're stuck.'

'Always!' said Cora.

They parted company at the foot of the tallest oak. Trix and Nis started up the spiral staircase to the Crow's Nest treetop cafe, while Cora and Jax continued on to the brook.

'Water fight?' asked Jax hopefully, as they rolled up their trouser legs and waded in.

'Fixing first, water fight after,' said Cora firmly.

'Boring snoring!' said Jax, accidently-on-purpose kicking water at Cora.

'Jax! Acorn head!'

'What? I'm cleaning the blanket!' Jax fished a pebble from the bottom of the brook and began to scrub at the dirt.

Cora giggled. Jax was a great friend. She stuck her hand in the brook and pulled out another pebble. 'I'll start at the opposite end.'

'Race you to the middle,' said Jax.

'You're on!' said Cora.

When the blanket was clean, they spread it over a bush to dry and then they started on the ladder. It wasn't as difficult as Cora had expected. Signor Dragonfly had taught them how to make bulrush ladders at school. To Cora's surprise, it all came back to her as she worked. When the ladder was finished, they tested it out, Jax climbing up a tree to hang it from a branch.

'Perfect!' said Cora when it was her turn to climb up, then down, the ladder. The job was good and she was almost bursting with pride.

By then the blanket had dried in the

sun and they set about repairing the holes. Sewing wasn't Cora's thing, nor Jax's, and they hadn't thought to ask Scarlet for needles and thread.

'Woodland magic?' Jax suggested.

Cora shot him a questioning look. 'Isn't that cheating?'

Jax blinked. He ran a hand through his long blue hair. 'Maybe a tiny peck. But Scarlet didn't say not to!'

Cora flexed her fingers. 'Woodland magic it is then!'

With a sparkly sprinkle of woodland magic, the holes were mended, leaving the blanket as good as new. Cora folded it carefully. It was time to face Scarlet.

They returned to the stores, where Haru and Scarlet were still putting things away.

Scarlet stopped tidying and looked expectantly from Cora to Jax.

Cora put the blanket on the counter
and Jax laid out the ladder. Scarlet breathed
in sharply, her nostrils quivering. First she
examined the ladder, tugging it to test its
strength, then hanging it from the top of the
store's door and climbing up and down it.

'Hmmm,' she said, moving on to the
blanket. She ran her hands over it, then
pressed it to her cheek. 'Hmmmm,' she said
again.

Cora held her breath.

'Wonderful work, you two, this is just the
ticket!'

Cora whooped, then clamped her hand
over her mouth. She stared at Jax, her eyes
shining. They'd got a '*just the ticket*'. It was
something Scarlet only said when she was
very, very pleased.

'Well and hmmm,' said Scarlet. 'You have
turned a bad nut good again. I am still not

happy that you took things from the stores
without my permission, but you were right
to help the young deer.'

'The bulrush ladder and the blanket will
be used twice now,' Haru added.

'Nothing is ever wasted by a Keeper!'
Scarlet agreed. She turned back to Cora and
Jax. 'One more successful expedition to the
Big Outside and then I will make you both
fully trained Keepers. Hop along now, before
I change my mind.'

Cora could hardly contain her relief and
excitement. She and
Jax hopped like
happy frogs all
the way out
of the stores,
where they joined
hands and spun
in a circle.

'Hurrah!' shouted Cora. 'No more school for us. Soon we'll be fully trained Keepers.'

'Rewilding the Big Outside for ever!' said Jax. 'Let's go tell Trix and Nis.'

'Let's celebrate with wild-strawberry muffins,' said Cora.

'And mushroom and garlic pizza,' said Jax.

'With daisy smoothies,' Cora added. 'Race you to the Crow's Nest!'

The End

✳ The Keeper Way ✳

Creating a Hedgehog Highway

Hedgehogs need to be able to travel
great distances at night to find food,
a partner and somewhere to nest. Most
hedgehogs cover around two kilometres
a night to do this. Unfortunately, new
developments, which provide us with homes
and other things we need, are making
it harder for hedgehogs to get around.
As a result, their numbers are falling. If

you have a garden, here's how you, and your neighbours, can help hedgehogs by providing them with a way to travel through your garden.

If you are making holes in fences, then ask an adult to help you. Please also remember to check if your house owns the garden fence before you cut a hole in it!

Things You Will Need
* A small saw
* A pencil
* Sandpaper

Building Your Hedgehog Highway

Decide which fence panel you want to use for your hedgehog highway. Ask an adult to remove the fence panel.

- At the bottom of the panel, draw an arch or square about 13 cm high.
- With the help of an adult, cut out the hole with the saw.
- Smooth any rough edges by rubbing them down with the sandpaper.
- Put your fence panel back and wait for the hedgehogs to travel through!

Walled Gardens

If you have a wall in or around your garden, you could ask an adult to help you knock a brick out of the bottom. You could also make wooden ramps and little staircases to help hedgehogs over structures such as steps or retaining walls that might be in their way.

More Ways to Help

Hedgehogs mostly eat bugs and fallen fruit, but the number of bugs has dropped and hedgehogs are often hungry. They also need water to drink and frequently suffer from dehydration. You can help hedgehogs to survive by leaving out a small saucer of tinned meaty cat or dog food and a shallow saucer of water. Specially made hedgehog food is also available to buy. Please do not leave out bread, milk or mealworms, as these are very bad for hedgehogs.

Julie Sykes

As a child, Julie was always telling tales.
Not the 'she ate all the cake, not me' kind,
but wildly exaggerated tales of everyday
events. Julie still loves telling stories and
is now the bestselling author of more
than 100 books for children of all ages
and is published around the world. She
has recently moved to Cornwall with
her family and a white wolf – cunningly
disguised as a dog. When she's not writing
she likes eating cake, reading and walking,
often at the same time.

Katy Riddell

Katy grew up in Brighton and was obsessed with drawing from a young age, spending many hours writing and illustrating her own stories, which her father (award-winning illustrator Chris Riddell) collected. Katy rediscovered her love for illustrating children's books after graduating with a BA Hons in Illustration and Animation from Manchester Metropolitan University. She loves working with children and lives and works in Brighton.

Protecting nature is magic for the secret little Keepers

The adventures of the Nature Keepers

Woodland Magic

FOX CUB RESCU

JULIE SYKES

illustrated by KATY RIDDELL

The adventures of the Nature Keepers

Woodland Magic

DEER IN DANGER

JULIE SYKES

illustrated by KATY RIDDELL

Woodland Magic

THE STRANDED OTTER

JULIE SYKES

illustrated by KATY RIDDELL

Look out for more adventures from the Nature Keepers.

Read on for an extract from
Woodland Magic: The Stranded Otter . . .

'Is it ready?' asked Cora.

A wooden raft lay on the bank of the stream that ran through the Hidden Middle of the Whispering Woods.

'Not quite.' Trix walked around the raft, occasionally stopping to tweak a vine or tighten a wooden screw.

'What's taking so long?' Jax asked.

'It has to be safe.'

Cora glanced at the other rafts already floating in the stream. None of them were as good as theirs. 'It won't sink, Trix. You're a genius,' she said proudly.

Cora and her friends Jax, Trix and Nis had finished their early morning rewilding tasks in the Big Outside and were working on their raft. Every year Grandmother Sky, the Queen of the Hidden Middle, celebrated her birthday with a raft race followed by a party by moonlight. It was the first time that Cora and her friends had been old enough to race and they couldn't wait. Trix, who loved making things, had designed the raft by herself.

Trix turned pink. She pushed her screwdriver into her bun for safekeeping and wiped her hands down her woven grass jeans. 'Let's get it in the water.'

The raft was made from a lattice of hollow reeds topped with a wooden platform. It had four bark seats, two at the front and two at the back. A leaf canopy, supported by twigs, gave the crew shelter from the sun or rain. Four wooden paddles were strapped to the deck with a vine.

Cora, Jax, Trix and Nis each stood at a corner, ready to lift it up.

'Hi, lo, go!' said Trix.

'Fizzing frogs, it's heavy!' Cora grunted. Her arms ached as she shuffled towards the water, carrying her corner of the raft.

'Jax, too fast,' Trix warned. 'We're not racing yet!'

'Sorry!' Jax slowed down.

When they reached the stream, Trix shouted instructions as they carefully lowered the raft into the water. A plaited vine rope allowed the raft to be tied to something on the bank, to stop it from floating away. Trix passed the rope to Cora. 'Hold this.'

The raft dipped as Trix stepped aboard. She untied the paddles and put one by each seat.

Cora held her breath and the rope. 'It floats!' she exclaimed when Trix was safely aboard.

A beaming Trix took her place at the back. Nis went aboard next, followed by Jax.

At last it was Cora's turn. She put a foot on the raft then stopped.

'Cattywumps! That poor caddisfly.'

A grey moth-like insect with hairy wings was floating on its back in the stream. Its legs waved feebly as it tried to right itself. Cora, one foot on shore, one on the raft, tucked the rope under her arm as she reached to rescue the caddisfly from the water. The raft drifted away from the bank. The gap between Cora's feet widened.

'Jump!' shouted Jax.

'Can't!' Cora's legs were doing the splits as the raft floated further away from the shore.

Jax knelt and held out his paddle to Cora. 'Hold the end and I'll pull you aboard.'

'What with?' Cora's hands were already full of caddisfly. The distance between the raft and the bank grew wider. Cora's legs were stretched as far as they could go. She cupped her fingers around the caddisfly and leapt for the bank. Her foot slipped as she jumped. Cora wobbled then fell. Splash! She landed in the water, dropping the vine but not the caddisfly. By holding her arm up she managed to keep the half-drowned insect out of the water. The stream was shallow enough for Cora to stand up in. Finding her feet, she waded to the bank, where she put the caddisfly on the grass to dry.

Was it still alive? A wing twitched. Cora's heart fluttered.

'Don't give up little one. I can heal you with some woodland magic.' Cora pointed her fingers at the caddisfly and imagined the insect growing strong again. She wiggled her fingers, showering its wings with a sparkly magical mist. A pip later, the caddisfly struggled up. Its wings quivered. Then it flew,

circling Cora, hovering in front of her nose
as if to thank her, before flying away.

Cora sighed happily. She loved all
animals, even the tiny ones.

'Well done, Cora,' From the raft, Jax,
Nis and Trix tapped their thumbs together,
congratulating her.

'Loser,' drawled a bored voice.

Cora looked up in surprise. Perfect
Penelope floated past, lounging on a raft
made from tree bark while her friend
Winnie paddled furiously with a wooden
oar.

'Eeew! Cora, you've got river weed
tangled in your hair. Oh no, silly me! That is
your hair.' Penelope cackled with laughter.

Cora ignored her. She didn't care if her
long green hair was wet and tangled. She'd
saved the caddisfly. That's what mattered.

Penelope didn't think so. 'I can't believe

you wasted woodland magic on an ugly caddisfly.' She shuddered.

'A waste, is it?'

Cora looked up to see Scarlet Busybee striding towards the stream, her face like a thundercloud. 'All bugs are important, no matter what they look like. Nature Keepers care for every living thing no matter how small or unusual. Do I make myself clear?' Scarlet's eyes bored into Penelope's.

Penelope stared at her feet. 'Yes,' she muttered.

'Hmmm.' Scarlet didn't sound convinced. 'Where is your paddle? Help Winnie bring that raft back to the bank immediately. It's not safe. It needs to be more stable before you can take part in the race.'

Scarlet then turned her attention to Cora. Tapping her thumbs together she said, 'Good work, Cora.'

Thank you for choosing a Piccadilly Press book.

If you would like to know more about our authors, our books or if you'd just like to know what we're up to, you can find us online.

www.piccadillypress.co.uk

And you can also find us on:

We hope to see you soon!